The Tales of
Kay and the Kitchen Friends

The Swim

By Piki Verschueren

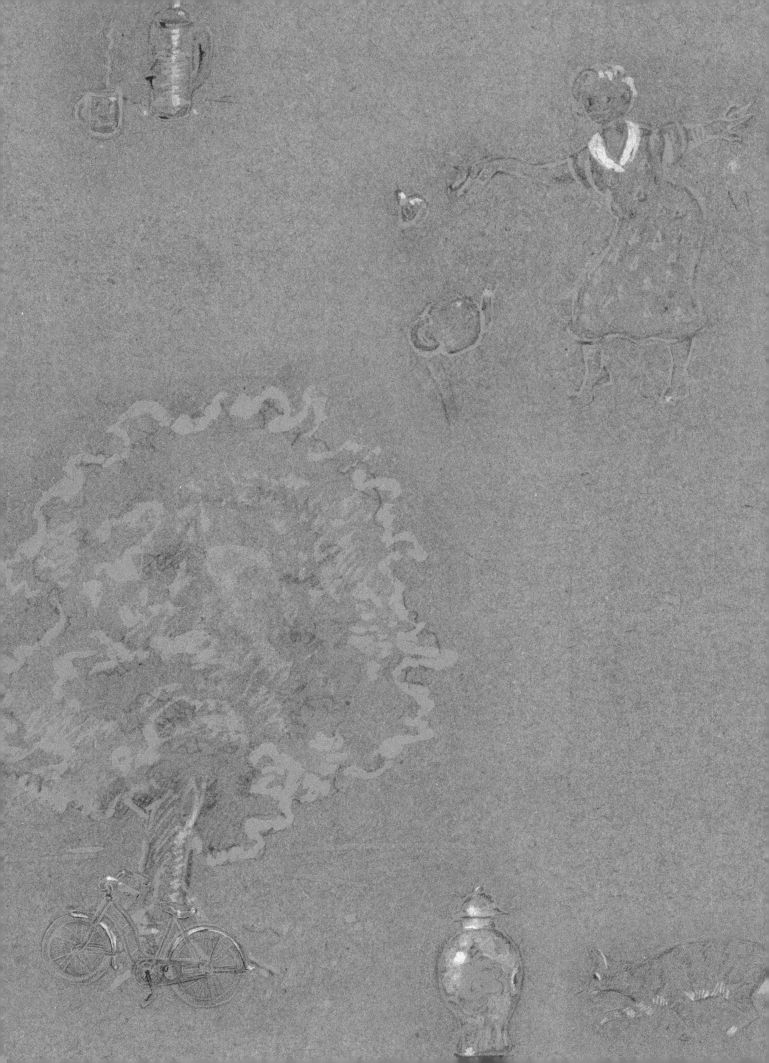

Illustrations and Text by Piki Verschueren
Text Editing by Jeremy Warner

Balboa Press books may be ordered through booksellers or by contacting:

Balboa Press
A Division of Hay House
1663 Liberty Drive
Bloomington, IN 47403
www.balboapress.co.uk
1 (877) 407-4847

Because of the dynamic nature of the Internet, any web addresses or links contained in this book may have changed since publication and may no longer be valid. The views expressed in this work are solely those of the author and do not necessarily reflect the views of the publisher, and the publisher hereby disclaims any responsibility for them.

Any people depicted in stock imagery provided by Getty Images are models, and such images are being used for illustrative purposes only.
Certain stock imagery © Getty Images.

ISBN: 978-1-9822-8034-5 (sc)
ISBN: 978-1-9822-8035-2 (e)

Print information available on the last page.

Balboa Press rev. date: 12/10/2018

BALBOA
PRESS
A DIVISION OF HAY HOUSE

The Tales of
Kay and the Kitchen Friends

The Swim

Kay was sitting quietly
on her chair,

when she suddenly heard
some yelling and loud chatter.

The noises were coming from the kitchen.
Kay got up to see what all the fuss was about.

She couldn't believe what she saw when she
gently pushed open the door. All the things
on the kitchen table giggled out loudly.

'Deary me,' she said firmly, 'what has gotten
in to you all? What is all this amusement
about? Have you lost all your manners?'

The kitchen things couldn't stop roaring and laughing.

'Hahahaha, hohohooo. The old jam jar just told us he would love to go for a swim in the pond. Fancy that. A jolly, tiny jam jar trying to swim. Impossible!'

On and on they went with their laughing and laughing.

Then all of a sudden, it was quiet again.

With a shy smile, teapot whispered, 'Kay, would you want to take us for a swim in the pond?'

So Kay packed them all a bit reluctantly but gently into her wooden crate. She strapped them tightly onto her bike, and off they went along the old cobblestone road to the pond.

A lovely warm summer breeze
blew gently over the surface of
the water. Bending over, Kay took
a deep breath, and hurled the
kitchen things into the pond.

'In you go, all of you!'

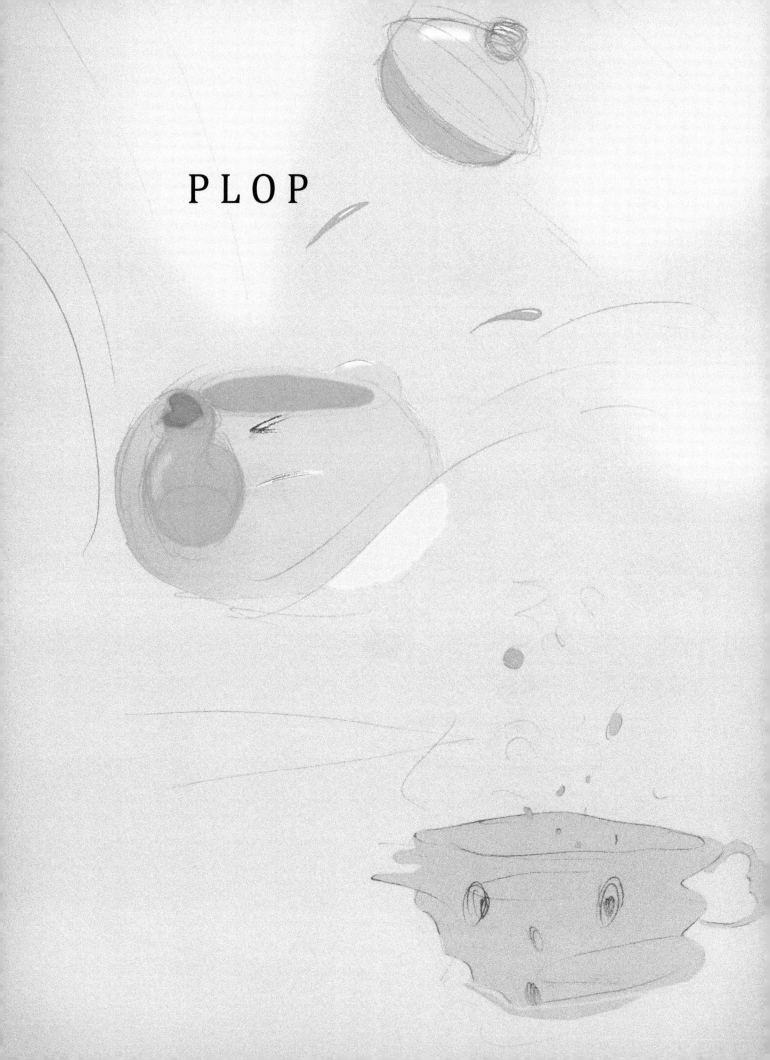

PLOP

SPLASH

The kitchen friends never swam before. But it seemed easy; they popped up right away to the surface.

They floated and floated and floated.

They floated for a long time.

Kay had a float too.

Whilst they were all gently bobbing up and down, they didn't notice three ducks approaching. They were on their way to have their daily swim.

'Oh look,' said one of them worriedly.
'Someone's littered our fine waters.'

'Good afternoon, lads,' quacked the biggest duck.

'You must be some sort of throwaways, am I right? We haven't seen species like you before. Is it possible that you lay eggs too?'

'Oh no,' muttered egg cup shyly. 'We don't lay eggs, but we do eat them for breakfast ... scrambled and boiled, runny and yolky.'

The big duck continued, 'Golly, how smashing that you should like eggs so much! Well, we will be having our monthly tea party with the Egg Hatchery Society this afternoon at the open meadow. Fancy a nice cup of tea to clear the old noggin? You're most welcome.'

Kay and the kitchen friends quickly dried
themselves and jumped eagerly onto
the bike to follow the three ducks.

It was hard to keep up with them.

When they finally arrived at the open meadow, they saw birds everywhere. Big ones, small ones, fat and tiny ones.

All around them flew feathers. The sky was full of cawing and cooing, chuckling and chattering, screeching and tweeting, jabbering and whistling and doodle-dooing! It was a marvellous concert, a symphony of twitter. And they all enjoyed this with countless cups of yummy hot tea.

Kay was very pleased to meet all these remarkable members of the Egg Hatchery Society.

'It is so nice to be here,' Kay said to the ducks after several cups of tea.

'But do I sense a slight hint of tension in the air?' she asked the birds cautiously.

'Quite right,' jabbered one of the ducks. 'How attentive.'

'You see, whenever we meet for our wonderful little tea parties, Mr Fox sneakily comes snooping, and when he gets his chance, he asks, "Good day to you folks. How do you do? Any chance that there's somebody here who wouldn't mind being eaten? I'm so hungry!"

Of course, every time we get together for a tea party, the thought of becoming a meal ourselves makes all our nerves jingle and jangle.'

'Oh dear,' said Kay with a sigh.

'Well, why don't you build a strong and sturdy camp to find shelter in when Mr. Fox sneaks up on you?' Kay suggested. 'I can lend you a hand.'

And so that's exactly what they did.
They built a camp as strong as a fort.

Every one of them
did their very best to
provide the sturdy
building materials
which were needed.

When the camp was built, they all sat in it for a while. It was a bit tight for space, but they all managed to squeeze in.

Soon enough, Mr Fox came along as expected.
Kay was vigilant. 'To what do we owe the
pleasure, Mr Fox?' she asked sternly.

'Well ... um ... I know it is such an
inconvenience to you kind folks, but is there
anybody here who wouldn't mind being eaten?
I really am so very hungry. I'm ravenous
as a lion,' Mr Fox responded politely.

'Mr Fox, it would be so very unkind if you ate one of us,' said Kay firmly.

'Here, have this instead,' she blurted,
grabbing the jam pot with both hands.

'But Kay', gasped the jam pot, 'why me?'

'Take the coffeepot or the milk pot.
Or better ... a mustard pot.

But please, please, not sweet, yummy jam me.'

Kay quickly put the jam pot down and opened the lid.

Mr Fox sniffed the jar before pushing
his nose down into the jam.

He had never smelled or tasted anything
like it before. It was a bit gooey, thick, and
juicy, and it had seeds. It tasted sweet and
fruity. Oh yes, he wanted it! All of it! And
he greedily gobbled it all up in one go.

'How very special! So sugary, so tasty,
so scrumptious indeed! Splendiferous!'

He thanked them all again and again.

'Goodbye for now. Toodle-oo!'

And the triumphant Mr Fox wandered
off the way he had come.

The afternoon sun had circled its way towards
the horizon. Thunder rumbled in the distance,
and soft raindrops soon pattered down on
the birds, Kay, and the kitchen friends.

Then the storm came in a great fury. The birds
scattered in every direction. Kay quickly grabbed
the whimpering and whining kitchen things
and threw them all back into the soap crate.

She pedalled home as fast as she could
against the wind, which was trying its best
to toss and turn everything in its path.

Martha, Kay's mum, waited anxiously for Kay to come home. She looked at her drenched daughter, who had dripped a trail of raindrops all over the floor.

'Why hello there, Kay, and where have you been all day?'

'We were at the Egg-Hatchery-
Society tea party, mummy.'

Martha looked at Kay with a frown on her face. 'Since
when do pots and pans go to tea parties, Kay?'

'I was very worried about you,' she said softly whilst finishing the washing-up.

'Well, Mums, I had the best day of my life,' replied Kay with glee.

And with that, they had a little supper and went to bed.

That night, some ducks flew swiftly back to their nests. They were very happy that they had met Kay and the kitchen friends that day.

In the meantime, a faint chuckling could be heard from the kitchen cupboard. 'Well, folks, I did have my swim, didn't I? And I do feel I am the bravest of jam jars ever, ever, ever … if I say so myself!'

What would have happened if Kay, the kitchen friends, and the birds hadn't built a camp together?

Have you ever built a
camp with friends?

Did you sleep in it?

You can draw jam pot here.

You can draw teapot here.

This book belongs to:

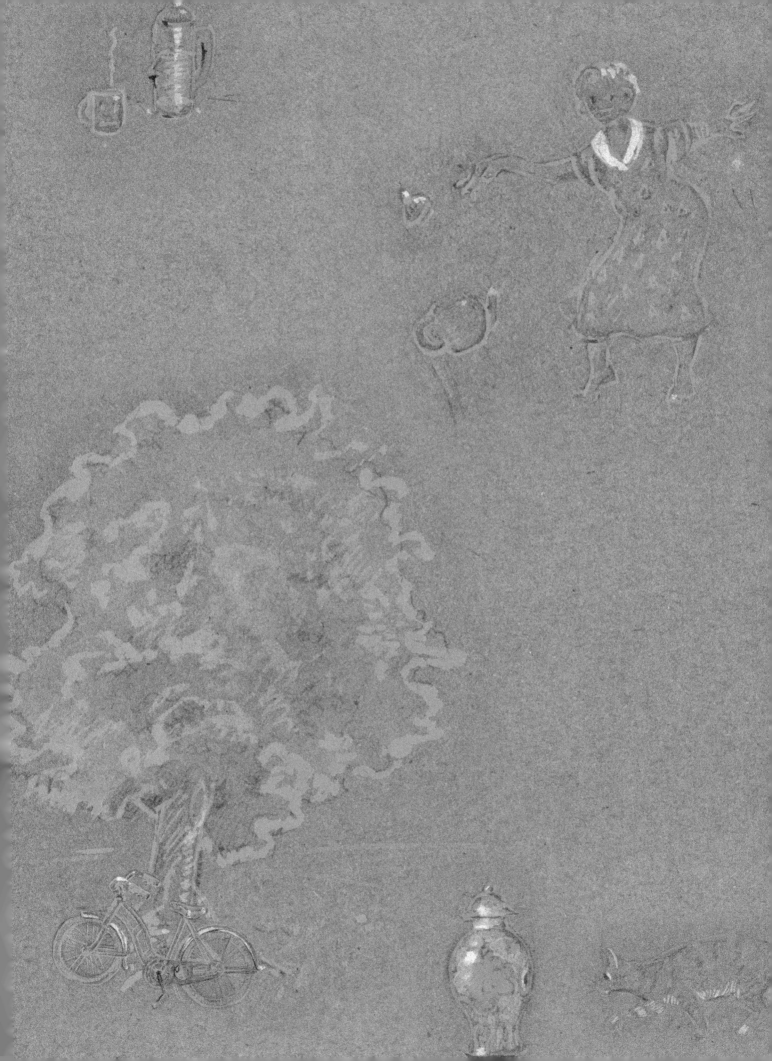

Lightning Source UK Ltd.
Milton Keynes UK
UKHW050702100119
335258UK00006B/85/P